# All My Friends

Gill Lobel
illustrated by Jo Blake

Tamarind

"I can't go to school today," said Keisha. "I've got a tummy ache." "Oh Keisha! Not again," sighed Mum. "All right, you can stay at home just for today."

Keisha snuggled down on the sofa.
She drew a picture of her best friend Olivia
at Mellor Road School, her old school.
Then she drew Mrs Jones.
She drew her curly hair and
her lovely smiley face.

Keisha sighed.
If only she could be back at her old school!

"Why don't you play outside in the fresh air?" suggested Mum. "You might feel better."

Keisha ran out into the yard.

She bent down to sniff a primrose.

Suddenly she saw something bright and shiny peeping out of the ground. Carefully she pulled it out.

"It's a little lady!" gasped Keisha.
The doll had a thin crack
running all round her waist.
Gently Keisha twisted...

Inside was a tiny doll
"I shall call you Little Katy and
Tiny Katy," she told the dolls.

The next morning Keisha slipped Little Katy into her pocket and held her tight.

Mum took Keisha all the way to the classroom.

"Hi Keisha!" Mrs Elliot smiled. "Come inside! I need someone to sort out the sea shells."

Keisha and Alpa sorted out
the shells together and
it was fun.

But at dinner time Alpa
ran off to play with Grace.
Keisha hid in a corner
with Little Katy.
"I don't care," she whispered.
Little Katy smiled back at her.

At home time, Mrs Elliot gathered
all the children around her.
"Tomorrow is Bring and Share Day," she said.
"I want you all to bring in something special
and tell everyone about it."

"I'm going to take my special school photo," Keisha told Mum. "The one with Mrs Jones and Olivia and all my friends."

Keisha kept her photo and
Little Katy safely in her pocket
all morning.

Then it was time
for P.E. in the hall.

Afterwards
Keisha got dressed quickly.
She slipped her hand
into her skirt pocket.

The photo was there,
but where was Little Katy?

"Keisha!" said Mrs Elliot. "Whatever are you doing?"

"Oh Mrs Elliot, she's gone!" sobbed Keisha.

"Who's gone, Keisha?"
"Little Katy's gone," cried Keisha.
Then she told Mrs Elliot about Little Katy and
about Olivia and Mellor Street School and
Mrs Jones.

Mrs Elliot turned to the class. "Keisha is feeling very sad," she said. "She needs good friends to help her find Little Katy."

"I'm Keisha's friend, Mrs Elliot," said Alpha. "I'll help!"

Everyone helped.

Suddenly Alpa gave a great shout.
"I've found her, Keisha! Just look where
she was hiding!"

"She must have rolled out of your pocket
when you got changed, Keisha," said Mrs Elliot.
Keisha cuddled Little Katy in her hands.
"Thank you," she said.

Then it was time for Bring and Share.
"Now, Keisha, what have you brought
for us?" asked Mrs Elliot.

Keisha looked at
her lovely photo.

Then she looked round
at all the smiling faces.
Slowly she put the photo
back into her pocket.

Very gently
she brought out Little Katy.

Then she told everyone her story.
"Little Katy was all sad and lonely in the garden.
Then I found her, and now she's my special friend.
And she has a secret – look!"

Keisha unscrewed Little Katy. "This is Tiny Katy.
She's so shy, she doesn't like to come out at all."

"But now she's got friends it's all right!"
Keisha laughed and looked around the class
at all the smiling faces, all her new friends.

ALL MY FRIENDS
TAMARIND BOOKS 978 1 848530 98 0

Published in Great Britain by Tamarind Books,
a division of Random House Children's Books
A Random House Group Company

This edition published 2009

3 5 7 9 10 8 6 4

Text copyright © Gill Lobel, 2006
Illustrations copyright © Jo Blake, 2006

The right of Gill Lobel and Jo Blake to be identified as the author and illustrator of this work has been asserted in accordance with the Copyright,
Designs and Patents Act 1988.

All rights reserved. No part of this publication may be reproduced, stored in a retrieval system, or transmitted in any form or by any means, electronic,
mechanical, photocopying, recording or otherwise, without the prior permission of the publishers.

TAMARIND BOOKS
61-63 Uxbridge Road, London, W5 5SA

www.tamarindbooks.co.uk
www.kidsatrandomhouse.co.uk

Addresses for companies within The Random House group Limited can be found at: www.randomhouse.co.uk/offices.htm

THE RANDOM HOUSE GROUP Limited Reg. No. 954009

A CIP catalogue record for this book is available from the British Library

Printed and bound in China

# OTHER TAMARIND TITLES

## FOR *All My Friends* READERS

Danny's Adventure Bus
Choices, Choices
Siddharth and Rinki
Big Eyes, Scary Voice
Caribbean Animals
South African Animals
A Safe Place
The Night the Lights Went Out
Time for Bed
Time to Get Up
Dave and the Tooth Fairy
Giant Hiccups

## BOOKS FOR WHEN YOU GET A LITTLE OLDER…

Amina and the Shell
The Dragon Kite
Mum's Late
Marty Monster
The Bush
The Feather
Princess Katrina and the Hair Charmer
Boots for a Bridesmaid
Starlight
Yohance and the Dinosaurs

## FOR BABIES

Baby Goes
Baby Noises
Baby Finds
Baby Plays

## FOR TODDLERS

Let's Have Fun
Let's Go to Playgroup
Let's Feed the Ducks
Let's Go to Bed
The Best Mum
The Best Blanket
The Best Toy
The Best Home

And if you are interested in seeing the
rest of our list, please visit our website:
www.tamarindbooks.co.uk